MICHAEL FIORI

Step Lovers

Taboo Erotic Romance

About the Publisher

4Fun Publishing, a member of **BLVNP Incorporated**, 340 S. Lemon #6200, Walnut CA 91789, info@blvnp.com / legal@blvnp.com
NOTE: Due to the highly emotional reaction of some people to works of erotic fiction, any email sent to the above address that contains foul language or religious references is automatically deleted by our anti-spam software and will not be seen. All other communications are welcome.

DISCLAIMER

Please don't be stupid and kill yourself. This book is a work of FICTION. Do not try any new sexual practice that you find in this book. It is fiction and not to be confused with reality. Neither the author nor the publisher or its associates assume any responsibility for any loss, injury, death or legal consequences resulting from acting on the contents in this book. Every character in this book is over 18 years of age. The author's opinions are not to be construed as the opinions of the publisher. The material in this book is for entertainment purposes ONLY. Enjoy.

Step Lovers
Taboo Erotic Romance

By: Michael Fiori

© **Michael Fiori 2015**
ISBN: 978-1-68030-295-0

"Kids, we are out the door in five -- get a move on!"

The Alberts were hours away from their long-awaited and much needed vacation, and Mrs. Albert was getting nervous that she couldn't hear the rolling of her son or daughter's suitcases on the floor upstairs yet. 'It's probably Hannah making sure she has every one of her fifteen thousand bathing suits,' thought Mrs. Albert as she checked her watch and went through her carry-on in the kitchen.

A moment or two later and she could hear at least one of her children making its way down the stairs. It was Mark by the sound of it -- at around 6'2" and 200 lbs., the solid young man's steps were unmistakable. He didn't need to pack nearly as much, just a bathing suit and some warm weather clothes.

"Rio De Janeiro, here we come!" Mark exclaimed as he rounded the corner to join his mother in the kitchen. His mother thought to herself, what a handsome boy he had become, and he looked it in his sweater and jeans, though he'd obviously need to change into something warmer when they arrived.

Mark's aunt had been suckered into one of those time-share sales pitches and ended up with a few weeks in a beautiful Rio beachfront home that they couldn't make time to use. So when they offered a week to Mark's family, the four had quickly agreed to take the vacation together. Rio de Janeiro was supposed to be beautiful in February, as opposed to the cold winter winds of the Midwest.

When Mark's dad joined his wife and son in the kitchen, it was time to yell at Hannah once again, who replied:

"I'M COMING!" from Hannah upstairs, in an annoyed tone. Hannah stopped briefly and grabbed the sexy pair of black laced panties she thought she might get to show to one of the vacationing boys she hoped to find there. Her brother would inevitably be staying out late banging some dim-witted college girls as she knew he's used to doing; why couldn't she have a little fun?

High school boys could be so frustrating. Hannah had a few times thought about giving her cherry to a boy she'd really liked, but they'd all disappointed her somehow. Whether it was bragging to their friends, or treating her badly to look cool... every one of them just wasn't worth it. But it was no wonder that they kept pursuing her -- Hannah is a stunner. She had deep green eyes with large black limbal rings around them, which looked almost animalistic when she was scolding her brother. Hannah's thick brown hair looked good straightened, as she usually wore it; or tossed up in a ponytail as it was when she headed downstairs. Her family finally saw her rounding the corner to the kitchen, wearing tight black yoga pants and an equally tight Yankees T-shirt over her 32C breasts.

"You don't even like the Yankees!" exclaimed Mark as his sister came into view. His eyes widened when he saw how little her outfit left to the imagination.

"Oh, shut up, Mark!" She got so frustrated with him sometimes. He was always picking on her, and though she sometimes liked it (it was like flirting practice for boys at school) he often got on her nerves, like now.

Mark couldn't help himself most times, she is an easy target. Plus, it helped him to distance himself in his relationship with his sister. He often felt bad how turned on he got when Hannah's friends came to visit or sleep over. As a senior in college, he wasn't supposed to find their teen bodies and their scantily clad nighttime appearances so arousing. They were his sister's age, and she was a battle unto herself.

Every so often, Mark thought maybe he could excuse his interest in her, hiding it behind the fact that they weren't 'technically' related. Their parents had married when both he and Hannah were very young, making them step-siblings. But they'd still grown up together, fought and played together, gone to school together... No, for all intents and purposes, Hannah was as much his sister as any of the annoying princesses, aka sisters, his buddies complained to him about. Only most of them didn't have to put up with one like his.

Hannah almost never covered up at home. Mark had more than once walked in on her naked and brushing her hair in the hall bath, causing her to jump and her tits to jiggle as she shrieked and he mumbled an apology. He was guiltily familiar with the particular shade of pink of his little sister's nipple that showed when her loose-fitting tank top had drooped during a lazy day on the couch. And seeing the sexy brunette's petite frame tanning on their deck with her bikini untied... it was sometimes too much.

So Hannah and her brother typically kept each other at a distance, which helped to calm some of the storms that can arise between two stubborn teens living together at home. Hannah's mother talked to her once or twice about being more discreet around her brother, but it still seemed like every other morning that he was seeing her cute pussy lips peeking out at him as she bent over to put makeup in the mirror and he swung open the un-closed bathroom door.

Once or twice, Mark had slipped into the unwitting fantasy of closing that bathroom door behind him and teaching Hannah a lesson or two about being naked around him, but his senses got the better of him. More than twice he'd found visions of her swimming around in his head as he released a little pent-up steam in bed at night, but those he shook as soon as he realized their presence as well.

And so, Mark did as he usually did when Hannah's tight ass had him wound up: he pushed the thought from his head, figuring that any 18-year-old with yoga pants hugging her cheeks the way Hannah's did would have his cock hardening the way it now was. His hardness made another appearance on the plane when Hannah's T-shirt rode up as she slept against the window, looking adorable. He gazed at her flat tummy before pulling the shirt down undetected. Brat or not, he didn't want the young guy in the next row checking out his little step-sister any more than he already was.

The family completed their travel about six hours after leaving the kitchen together, and they were tired. That long trip, cooped up in an airline seat or the back of the uncomfortable resort bus left all four family members longing for a nap before they arrived early afternoon. Hannah was the first to go for it after they'd ooohed and ahhhhed over the beauty of their temporary home. She pulled her T-shirt over her head as she sauntered down the hallway, revealing a comfortable cotton bra that Mark's eyes couldn't miss before she closed the door behind her and laid down on the soft bed.

Mark went to his own bedroom and dozed off to the image of his sister's backside burned into his eyelids: her wiry arms prying the skin-tight cotton tee off her body and the flexing of her beautiful back as she lifted her arms over her head... it simply wouldn't leave him until he was fast asleep. Even then it was Hannah's body that pervaded his dreams as he napped, his own little sister causing his cock to stand at attention for the better part of an hour or two before:

KNOCK KNOCK KNOCK

Mark rubbed his eyes and let out a yawning mumble, "Yeah. I'll be there in a minute!"

"Come on, sleepyhead," squealed Hannah

Mark got out of bed and went to the door, his sister didn't seem like she was going to let up until he showed her he was out of bed. When he came to the door and cracked it open so light streamed onto his face, his little sister stood there on the threshold with her hip cocked, looking hot as ever. She was all prepped and ready to go, hair pulled back with a pair of sunglasses atop it, a yellow spaghetti-strap top holding up her beautiful rack, and jean shorts so short he could see the pockets peeking from below the tattered hem. She had obviously been working on her tan leading up to the vacation, and it made every inch of exposed skin a magnet for her brother's eyes.

'What the hell, man!' Mark thought as he rubbed sleep from his eyes, 'We've only been here an hour or two and you're already gawkin' at your own sis!' Mark had suspected Hannah was going to be showing off a bit when they got on vacation. She was starting to develop that curiousness that highschool girls have, when boys were checking her out everywhere she went. He didn't expect, however, to be one of those guys himself, but it was happening regardless. Thoughts wandering, he readied himself and by the time he emerged, his family was already walking out the door.

"Where are we headed anyway?" Mark called after his mom as he closed the front door behind him.

"Well," she replied, "since we always wait to go into town 'til the last day, and your father and I explored the grounds while you two were wasting time napping, we figured we'd go see what downtown has to offer."

Mark and Hannah beamed at her suggestion; they both figured they'd be more likely to find a cute boy or girl there rather than the resort. But Mark found one sooner than that; on the bus to the town's main street, a desirable-looking brunette caught Mark's eye and seemed to be sitting alone. Mark got up from his seat and approached her; he'd only just sat down next to Hannah and he figured she wouldn't mind. He cracked a joke and politely asked to join her and before long, the two of them were smiling and chatting like old friends.

Hannah did mind, however. Mark's new seat had left her feeling awkwardly alone. Her parents in the row in front of them were flirting in that weird way they sometimes did, and it made Hannah want to gag. Instead, she turned her head and decided to get a better look at the girl Mark had found.

'That's just like him,' she thought with a twinge of anger. But it wasn't anger that struck her as she eyed up the new flavor of the week, it was jealousy, and it was causing her to start comparing the brunette's attributes to her own. 'My tits are definitely better than hers,' she thought begrudgingly, her hands made their way to her own breasts, feeling them to be sure. 'And she's not in shape at all,' she kept spinning. By the time they arrived downtown, she had analyzed every part of the girl without even realizing it and was sure she was prettier in every way. But then, like her brother, she had to scold herself for getting so worked up over her brother's new friend. Hannah thought maybe she just needed something to eat to cure her crankiness.

But her wrath didn't stop there, or at the dirty look she gave the new girl as she stood giggling with her brother as they stepped off the bus. Mark's parents were prepared to give him a minute as they checked out the downtown, and then maybe let him go off on his own, but Hannah had no such plans.

"Daaaaddd, I want to go try on some clothes, can you ask Mark to come with me?"

"Honey, he's busy, I'm not going to interrupt him while he's talking to his new friend," her father replied. "Just come with your mother and me to this art gallery and then we'll go wherever you want."

"No way, I know how long I could end up looking at some silly painting with you two! I'll just go alone."

"Oh no you don't, Hannah," he retorted immediately, but she was already headed away from him and pretended not to hear. Her father then called after her: "You can't go anywhere around here alone!" But it was no use, she was obviously cranky and he knew that she wasn't going to listen to him when she was acting like that. So Mr. Albert, with a sorrowful look on his face, interrupted his son's conversation with the pretty girl and explained he'd need to run after his step-sister and be her bodyguard until she came around. Mark huffed and hawed, but in a few seconds, agreed to meet Emily, whose name he'd just learned later that night and took off after his sister.

"Hannah, wait up!" He said as he was about 30 feet behind her. She was about to turn the corner so he hustled and caught up to her.

"What's gotten into you Hannah, why didn't you answer me? I know you heard me." Mark asked as he grabbed her arm and she finally stopped her long strides.

"Well, excuse me; I didn't think it could be you calling me. You were so busy with that skanky looking girl you met on the bus; I didn't think you'd have found the time to come after me."

Hannah nearly winced as she said the words. She realized as they came out that they were a bit harsh, and she shouldn't be acting so jealous; it was only her brother after all. She looked up at him; her eyes had been fixed on her feet. Mark didn't see a scowl as he'd expected after that outburst, but a hesitant smile. He knew the look well; it was always his favorite way of avoiding a fight with her. So he put on a big smile and Hannah began to giggle as she always did when she realized she was being crabby.

"Let's get you something to eat," Mark said as he took her hand and they turned back in the direction Hannah had been heading. "But don't think I'm going to sit around while you try on ten thousand hats like we did in Mexico."

Hannah laughed as she remembered it, happy that her brother had joined her and left the bimbo who'd been stealing all his attention. She didn't like to admit it, but even though she and her brother had the occasional explosive fight, there was nothing like a good laugh with him; it cheered her up immediately.

Before long, the two siblings were casually rambling the streets of the admittedly dingy town, though the delicious pastry Hannah was snacking on was a thing of wonder. As she felt the sugary sweetness touch her lips for the first time, she began to feel better; or maybe it was her brother's arm around her that did it. She could see why girls liked him. He was handsome and smart, and he was so good at making her feel the way she did now: happy.

At a sleepover one night, one of her friends had suggested that Mark looked like Jake Gyllenhaal, and though she'd said she didn't see it, she had probably watched every movie he'd been in twice since. Once again, she felt grateful she'd pried him away from the other girl.

So they went on, walking and talking with Mark poking fun at Hannah for the pockets of her jean-shorts showing and Hannah clinging to her brother's arm like a child. At one point, with his arm wrapped around her, Mark felt the hem of her shirt rise up and his hand fell upon bare skin. He knew he should have moved it, but when Hannah didn't say anything he decided against it. Besides, it was an innocent touch, like the way his fingers moved all by themselves and pried at the waist of her shorts daringly. He must have just been feeling a bit turned on by the girl his sister had successfully twat-blocked him from.

They stopped in to a few interesting looking stores; Hannah tried on a hat at one of them to get a rise out of her brother and the shopkeeper threw them out when they bumped into a display as he grabbed it from her head. At one point, Hannah convinced her brother to come into a store with all kinds of clothing displayed outside. He sighed and ducked under a low-hanging wind-chime as he followed his sister in the store. She pranced about a bit, looking at this and that before going to the changing room to try something on.

Mark had his back turned when Hannah came out.

"What do you think?" She said as Mark turned to face her. She stood posing in the same jean shorts, but an entirely different top. It looked to be knitted, probably by the woman standing at the entrance to the store, and it wasn't quite opaque. It didn't hardly cover half of her upper body, stopping halfway up her abdomen. He could see tiny gaps in the woven fabric throughout, with Hannah's chest peeking through at him. When he noticed the dark pink circles atop her perky breasts, he looked away.

"Hannah, I think I can see a little too much through that!" He exclaimed.

"Oh settle down you dog, I'll wear something underneath it, I just want your opinion."

"It looks real nice Hannah," Mark assured, looking at her kind-of sideways.

His eyes stopped for a moment and Hannah looked down to see what he saw. One of her nipples had found its way through the fabric and was poking through clearly. She shrugged her shoulders and said:

"Ooops, maybe you're right," twitching a bit as she tucked the nub beneath the fabric and closed the door to the changing room. She felt a bit naughty revealing herself like that to her step-brother, but it wasn't that different from what he got at home -- this time has been just a bit more... obvious, she supposed.

"Alright already," she called to him, having redressed herself and emerged from the changing room, "you can look now Mr. Righteous." She gave him a snooty look and walked to the door to pay for her new shirt. Mark noticed immediately that she had folded her yellow top half-way up and under, and his wide eyes gave him away.

"Jeez, what are you, my dad?" She probed him, "It's hot out here and unless you want to see me sweating, I'm going to fold up my damn shirt."

"Wow, okay," he said, backing off, "I was just worried the midriff-monster had gotten to you in the changing room."

"Ugh," she breathed, walking out of the store with her cute new purchase, she couldn't wait to try it on later.

They kept on roaming about until Mark finally said, "we should probably think about heading back, it's got to be two hours since we left mom and dad."

Hannah didn't look pleased, but she agreed and they turned to go back and meet their parents. However, as they made their way back, something caught Hannah's eye. Down a side street, beyond a dark stretch of road there was a sign that said simply, "ANTIQUES," and it was probably a hundred feet from anything resembling a store. 'What an odd place for an antique store,' she thought inwardly, 'and that is definitely the first sign I've seen in a while written in English,' her brain hinted. She felt oddly drawn toward it.

"Mark, come on, check this out," she said, grabbing his hand and pulling him off their intended path.

"What is it now Han'?"

"Look at this place! Why do you think it's it so far from everything else," she said with childlike wonder in her eyes. It was cute, and Mark decided against ruining her parade and instead followed her lead, even if the alley did give him the creeps.

They passed a few doors to what were probably garages on the other side, and an abandoned old barber shop before they were standing beneath the buzzing, neon sign. The window panes were cloudy and the inside was only dimly lit, but he had to admit -- it was intriguing. Mark was just contented to look through the storefront, but Hannah would have none of it, and once again he was treated with a view of her denim-hugged behind as she pranced into the store.

"Greetings children..." Mark practically jumped as the old woman sitting behind a very old-looking desk spoke to them. Her face was only lit by a small desk lamp, but it didn't look pretty. In fact, it looked exactly as he might have expected to, like the croaking voice that had come from her old, dry lips.

"What can I help you with, my dear?" asked the old woman in the direction of his sister.

The place may have crept Mark out, but Hannah seemed entirely unfazed, as was her nature.

"Oh, nothing," she beamed, "we're just bored and we saw your shop from way down the street."

"Ahh yes," croaked the old lady, "many years ago this was the busiest street in town, but not anymore. Perhaps I can find something to cure your boredom young girl, why don't you and your boyfriend follow me!"

Mark was about to protest, but Hannah gave him a look that suggested he ought to just let that one slide. So they followed the old woman further back into the shop, into a small alcove created by three enormous armoires, each with hundreds of tiny drawers. A small, square window above them cast a dim light on a table directly in the center of the alcove; dust particles lingered listlessly in the air.

Hannah turned to her brother with an excited grin; perhaps Hannah had finally led him somewhere that didn't involve pastel colors or pretty beads this time. The two siblings waited anxiously as the old woman fumbled through a few drawers near the middle of one armoire.

Out of the drawers she'd chosen, the old woman drew three glass vials. Each held a liquid of slightly different color, with a thick, syrupy appearance.

"Bored you say?" she asked. "Try one of these and I promise all your boredom will melt away! Place three drops of this green elixir in a cup of tea before bed, and you'll find your dreams utterly at your control." As she described it, she held the vial to the light and the two

Albert children found their eyes glued to it. "A touch of this red one to your tongue, and you'll find any food tastes one thousand times better, if only for a few moments.

Once again, she held it to the light and their eyes fixed on the pearlescent appearance of the liquid. Hannah was positively speechless, but the reasonable side of Mark finally found himself wondering how much the old coot was going to charge for what was probably sugar-water as she set the second vial beside the first.

The old lady hesitated, looking down at the last vial in her hands. It was much smaller than the first two, with a pretty crystal stopper and a jet black liquid inside.

"What does that one do?" Hannah questioned her impatiently.

The old lady didn't answer at first, looking up at the two young ones before her and then back at the vial in her withered palm. "My dear, who did you say you two were again, I can be very forgetful?"

When Hannah didn't speak up, Mark chimed in quickly, feeling a bit wary of the question, "We're brother and sister, and we're here with our parents staying at a resort near the coast."

"How nice," replied the old woman, closing her bony fingers over the vial, "then perhaps I have just the thing for you." She quickly rustled through a drawer nearest her and pulled from it a vessel just like the other two sitting on the table. The smaller vial she put back in its original drawer, except she inserted a key into the tiny lock above its numbered plate and turned it to seal the drawer shut.

"But wait!" cried Hannah, "you didn't tell us what that one did!"

"Sorry, my dear, but this one's not for sale."

Hannah didn't look pleased with her answer, but when the old woman denied her access to it again as she described the third potion, Hannah seemed to drop it. Apparently this blue liquid could let them hold their breath underwater for up to ten minutes -- one use only. Mark was starting to feel claustrophobic in the tiny antiques shop, and he felt the need to hurry them along.

"How much for all three?" he queried.

"Because you two have brightened an old woman's day, how about.... Fifty real. That's twenty five dollars if you have it

Mark was surprised, and paid the old lady eagerly after following her to the front of the store with his little sister in tow. As they made their way to the desk, Mark saw the old lady hang the key on a tiny nail that had been tapped into the side of one chest of drawers. He hoped Hannah didn't get any ideas, but when he reached behind him to grab his wallet and didn't see his step-sister there as well, he was almost certain she had.

"Excuse me, ma'am, I think I may have dropped my cell phone back there, do you mind if I go back and grab it?" He asked politely, handing her some folded bills from his wallet. The old lady permitted him, wave her hand and mumbled something about kids and their cell phones, before rustling through her money box to make changes. Mark ducked around to the back of the store in a flash, but not fast enough to catch Hannah before she'd already gotten up to no good

The key was missing from its hanging spot. In fact, it was now hanging from the keyhole in the exact drawer he'd hoped it wasn't. Hannah was turned away from him, holding up the flask to the light like the elderly woman had done before.

"Hannah," he whispered, coming to her side to scold her.

He saw her jump, and before he knew it, the tiny vial had slipped from her hands and crashed down upon the wooden tabletop. As soon as it landed, the liquid disappeared in a puff of fragrant smoke. It smelled.... wonderful. Was that hazelnut, his favorite flavor? Or was it lavender, like the body wash he so often smelled on Hannah fresh out of the shower.

Hannah took in the scent too, distracted from the enormous mistake she'd just made. The smoke snaked into her nostrils and filled her with the scent of.... Mmmm... The pine trees she'd smelled on the mountaintop in Colorado last year when the family had gone skiing, But there was also the scent of old leather, like that of the boxing gloves and bag she loved watching her brother use to work out.

"Okay, my dears, I've wrapped your purchases up as best I could, I hope you enjoy......" As the old woman turned the corner and saw the two siblings standing over the broken flask, she knew exactly what had happened. She cursed herself for leaving the key in its usual spot; she should have known that the curious brunette wouldn't leave it alone.

"Out with you! OUT!" She cried, "You don't know what you've done.... I TOLD YOU IT WASN'T FOR SALE."

Mark grabbed Hannah's hand and pulled her past the old woman with a stammering apology. In a few seconds, he'd whisked his little sister through the store and out the front, her thick brown hair trailing behind her as they went. They had to leave their potions behind; he doubted they'd have worked anyway. The old woman called after them as Mark and Hannah galloped down the street.

"FOOLS, CARELESS LITTLE FOOLS THE BOTH OF YOU!" she squawked, coughing after the effort.

She may have said something else but neither of the two could distinguish it as they emerged from the alley. Mark thought he heard her say: "get far away from each other," halfway through her sentence, but that couldn't have been it. Hannah bent at the waist to catch her breath and Mark put a hand on her lower back. They both laughed, and laughed; it had truly turned out to be an interesting morning.

"I can't believe you just did that Han," he shot at her, still giggling, "I mean, what if that old witch had put a hex on you or something?" He joked.

"Didn't I say we should go down that street!" she beamed proudly. "But we have to go back for our potions!"

"Come on Hannah, you don't actually believe any of that nonsense do you?"

Hannah bumped him with her hip and reluctantly sided with him as they headed back in the direction of the center of town. But even as she agreed with her brother, his hand upon her waist felt slightly different; perhaps it was just the fact that she'd rolled up her shirt and his strong palm was now completely upon her bare flesh.

No, that wasn't it. As she walked along, her head began to feel light, her body almost weightless. She stopped walking and put a hand to her head. Even before he spoke, she could sense him there, her big brother questioning: "Hannah, is everything okay?"

"Yeah dork, I'm fine, just a little winded from our escape."

"Looks like someone needs to work out a little more," he mocked, then surprised her by spanking her butt daringly. She wasn't sure why she didn't lash out at him; she usually would have.

The place where he'd touched her on her butt cheek felt sensitive, ticklish almost as she started walking again. She nuzzled closer to her brother, not knowing that the potion was working in spite of her.

But whatever it was, it hadn't hit Mark yet, him being bigger and harder to dose. However, he couldn't help but enjoy the feeling of his arm wrapped around his little sister's taut abdomen. He had, at times, admired how strong she kept her core. He'd seen it so many times when she came home from the gyp, always looking incredible in her sports bra and tiny workout shorts.

But after probably ten more steps he began to feel it too, whether he knew it or not. His fingers depressed into Hannah's soft side on their own, stretching as if to gather more flesh. When she stopped moving to catch her breath and his hand slid from her, Mark suddenly wished he could put it back. He watched her as she leaned against the wall and looked away from him.

Hannah was feeling a bit frightened by it, by the sudden feelings she could only describe as horniness. But it wasn't for just anyone; it was for the attractive young man that was now touching her cheek to calm her down. He could tell by her breathing that she was wound up about something, but he could not have seen that kiss coming as he turned her face to his.

Hannah! What do you think you're doing?" He asked, the potion still fighting to control him.

But Hannah didn't answer him, she just looked at him lustfully, similar to the way he'd seen her look when she was inspecting the potion that was now working its way through their bodies. And she stayed there against the wall, turning so both her shoulder blades made contact with the cool brick wall. She arched her lithe body so her hips met Mark's; he was standing entirely too close.

And then, as if on their own, Mark's hands found the exposed sides of Hannah's abdomen as it thrusts toward him. He leaned into her, his front lining up with Hannah's as his hands got bolder. At first they just squeezed at her flexed ABS, marveling at the wonderful firmness of them. But within seconds they had jumped all the way to her breasts, those wonderful globes he'd been denying himself for years. When they landed there, his lips were magnetized to Hannah's and they locked again in a feverish kiss, this time with both of them on board.

With their lips mashed and their tongues entwined, the two siblings felt each other in ways no sibling is supposed to, and it was wonderful. Hannah's tits, covered only by the tiny spaghetti strap shirt, felt glorious in Mark's hands. He massaged them and pinched at her nipples through the cotton. Hannah moaned into his mouth.

"Oh God Hannah," Mark said, pulling away from their kiss a few inches, "what are we doing?"

Again Hannah didn't speak; she just stared into his eyes as he kept his hands motionless atop her breasts. Hannah's gave Mark's cock, hardened since their first kiss, one more push with her hips and Mark flinched with a hopeless look on his face. Wordlessly, the pretty little brunette descended slowly to her knees, and though it was her first time, she gracefully opened Mark's pants and reached inside.

It was all happening too fast. Mark had not but a few seconds to interrupt his step-sister's actions and when he felt her tiny hand wrap around his shaft, the decision was made for him. He could only watch... watch as Hannah worked his dick through his pants and out into the open. He could only watch as she admired it, pointing directly at her mouth and within seconds -- engulfed it.

Hannah choked a little bit as she took her brother's hard length into her mouth. It was warm and so thick that she had to open wide to fit it. After sucking gently at the first few inches of him, she took Mark's tip to her pursed lips and kissed it, following the peck with the lapping of her tongue. Her saliva coated him and when she was satisfied with his shiny helmet, she looked up at him and locked his gaze. Slowly she pressed his tip through her lips and into her mouth. She kept going though, and before long she had taken half of his cock into her mouth, eyes still holding his.

She pressed a bit further and felt him make contact with the back of her throat. Hannah gagged and withdrew, and once she had slipped him from her mouth again she smiled proudly at how obviously her stepbrother was enjoying the treatment. So she continued it, sucking and bobbing her head toward the base of his cock. Mark looked around; his little step-sister was blowing him in the middle of a side-street, and he could hear people moving about in the town square nearby.

Somewhere a street performer strummed a guitar, but the sound was far overpowered by that of Hannah slurping at his penis in her mouth. This went on for a few moments, but Mark wished it would never end. His worries of being discovered melted away with each following plunge of her mouth around his cock.

Hannah could have stayed like that until he released a big load into her mouth, feeling as if she'd enjoy the taste him on her tongue. But it was not to be, for Mark pulled her to her feet and was kissing her once more before she even had time to catch her breath. The elixir finally coursing its way through him from head to toe, Mark had but one mission. He took the bottom of Hannah's folded shirt in his fingers and pried it up over her head.

Her breasts jiggled free, defying gravity as she held her arms over her head with her beautiful pink nipples standing at attention. He put a hand against one and another to the button at the waist of her tiny jean shorts. In less than a second he had them unbuttoned and his free hand was pushing both shorts and panties down Hannah's long, fit legs. They bunched at the bottom, and Mark could see that Hannah had been wearing yellow cotton panties to match her top, now bunched beneath them on the cobblestones.

It didn't take much for Hannah to push her step-brother's pants down the rest of the way, and then they both stood there in the street, naked as the day they were born and obviously about to fuck.

Mark looked around, not out of the fear they'd be discovered, but in search for somewhere to fuck Hannah properly. An abandoned food cart with an old piece of canvas thrown over it provided the perfect spot. So, strong as he was, Mark lifted the naked little brunette up and she wrapped her legs around him. They kissed in their standing position, with Mark's cock pressed firmly against Hannah's dripping pussy while they did. Slowly he moved her over to the spot, not wanting to disrupt her eager playfulness as she nibbled on his lips and tongue.

Her soft cheeks made contact with the canvas and Mark set her weight down upon the cart hastily, eager for what would come next. They both paused.

Mark's rod pointed directly toward the place they both wanted it: inside Hannah's inviting little pussy, and soon with one last ounce of resistance shown upon each sibling's face, Mark looked down to see what he was about to do, the forbidden act he was about to commit with his little step-sis. He gazed up at Hannah; her beautiful body was sprawled out in front of him with her pink pussy waiting for him to push passed her puffy lips and take it.

Two bystanders down the road walked by and saw them, one of them looked twice when he saw what was going on down the street and quickly gossiped to a woman who was walking alongside. Mark felt a pang of guilt along with the heat of Hannah's opening when his tip touched against it.

"Mark.... be gentle, I'm a virgin."

That did it, if there was any hope of stopping before, the sweet words of his step-sister both revealing her secret and inviting him to wash it away had him entering her without another word.

His head split her tiny lips.

"Oh Mark.... unhhhhhhh" gasped Hannah.

He continued pushing into her ever so slowly, encountering resistance.

"Hannah, take my hand, this might hurt a little," Mark warned her. She wrapped her fingers around his and Mark's other hand supported her back. Mark knew they may have onlookers, but taking Hannah's virginity seemed much more important to him then. He urged forward, feeling her hymen tear in every push. Mark saw the teen wince in pain as the forbidden penetration took place. She squirmed underneath him, wiggling about his impaling cock.

He went on further. Another person had slowed down to see what was going on by the abandoned cart, though it was obvious once Hannah let out an adorable squeal. Her brother had only just breached her hymen and she already felt so full. Hannah couldn't see the onlooker, but it wouldn't have made any difference to her, she was fixed on being manhandled by Mark and she had no plans to turn back. Mark might have done something differently if the potion hadn't tossed his inhibitions to the wind.

"Are you okay Han, do you want me to take it out?" Asked Mark, his voice laden with compassion. Hannah settled down a bit.

"No!" she quickly replied, feeling him withdraw a fraction of an inch -- he stopped immediately, "I only need a second.... mmmmmmn..... owwwww... It's just really big Mark..."

Halfway buried in her pussy, Mark was afforded a second to gather his thoughts. Something had obviously changed between the two of them, and he was almost certain the old woman had not been brewing sugar-water in her dank old store. But the earlier feelings of guilt weren't there anymore, and despite that he knew he shouldn't currently be immersed in his little step-sister's quim, it didn't change the fact that he loved the feeling and wanted more. He had only entered her, but an inch, and she already felt unfathomably tight.

"Okay Marky, go slow." Hannah begged. Her brother smiled at the pet name she sometimes used and snapped back to the reality that it was his step-sister asking him to start fucking her again.

They both looked down at Mark's shaft, half buried in Hannah's pussy and ready to go all the way. He began to push more of it into her, so slowly that Mark could feel his patience being tested. What he wanted to do was to feel Hannah's legs wrapped around him as he drove into her with satisfying and forceful thrusts, but it would have to wait.

Hannah's face still showed that her body was adapting to Mark's size, and though he could see her enjoying it, he didn't want to ruin the moment. Instead, he leaned in and kissed her, distracting her as he sank the rest of his cock slowly into her.

The anxious eighteen-year-old felt her worries subside as her step-brother penetrated her, relieved that the pain of losing her virginity had not been too great.

Mark was planted there, kissing her with their hips connected below. Hannah couldn't control her breathing from the unfamiliar feeling of being filled so deeply; her entire abdomen had expanded along the length of his cock within. She was unfathomably wet, wetter than any girl Mark had been with before. His hand cupped her face as her eyes widened due to the intense feeling of her brother's fully invading member.

"mmmmmnnnhhh," she moaned into his open lips.

His tongue teased her big, red lips. He could taste the strawberry chapstick she always wore on them. Mark savored the kiss as he slowly withdrew his cock and Hannah moaned again. Thankfully, her lithe little body had prepared her teenage tunnel for Mark's cock with her wetness, for it hurt her far less than she'd imagined. She was eager for her him to sink into her again when he said:

"Are you sure you're okay Hannah? I don't want to hurt you."

She nibbled at his lower lip and then pecked a few quick kisses on him with pursed lips; Mark loved the way she played with him.

"I'm sure big brother, you can fuck me now I think," she replied, pulling away from his face and wearing a naughty, come-hither grin.

Mark would never have admitted it until the potion came along, but his dreams were frequently visited by his gorgeous step-sister, sometimes in the very position she now lay. He couldn't have even dreamed, however, of taking Hannah's virginity, a thought which made the next thrust into her all the sweeter.

Suddenly filling her in one deliberate thrust, Hannah truly experienced the feeling of being fucked by her step-brother. As his shaft slid between the squeezing walls of her pussy, she could feel a tingle run all through her body and cause her mind to temporarily flood with light-headed bliss. When he bottomed out in her, and his head had reached further into her than she thought possible, her vision blurred.

"Ohhmygodd Mark, keep going...mnhhh.... do it again," she encouraged him.

Withdrawing, he instinctively palmed the hipbones of his eighteen-year old step-sister's tiny waist. As he'd wished, he could feel her soft soles waiting for him to pull all the way out before urging him back in. They watched, entranced, as the shaft revealed more and more until her clinging pink lips released Mark's tip. It looked glistening wet.

Hannah drew a breath to ready herself and Mark dove back into her at a needier pace. Now that he had been inside her once, no twice... he had to be snugly inserted again. He wanted to bury deep into her and hear her squeal with delight as he tickled her deeper than he ever had during the wrestling matches they still got into that day.

And when he did she rewarded him with that and more:

"Ohhh, Ohhfuck --" she winced, "OhhhhmyGoddd!" He had reached somewhere that made his little step-sis writhe upon his deeply penetrated rod. "Keep fucking me like that Mark," she gasped on as he hesitated, then buried inside her.

Mark pulled out of the little brunette and sank into her again, and again, and again -- it was exactly what Hannah wanted. Before long he had worked them both into a tangle of pawing and touching and attempts to urge Mark deeper into her if it was possible.

The sun only struck the wall across the street about a quarter of the way down and they may have been in shadow, but a small group had stopped walking momentarily to be sure they were really seeing what they thought they saw.

Hannah didn't hear them until a younger woman in the group giggled aloud, but as she saw them and then looked back at her step-brother, she pleaded in the cutest way she could muster:

"Don't stop," he thrust into her again, "please" she whispered as Mark thudded against her mound and her tits shook, "don't you stop." Her puppy dog eyes shone brightly.

He didn't. Mark felt as Hannah did: that the forbidden nature of their lovemaking was only made more exciting by the fact that they were doing it on the street, where anyone could see them. For all they knew, their parents could walk past that very street by chance and see Hannah and Mark locked in loving embrace.

"What if our dad came walking around that corner... ooooouhhh… huh Mark?" He slid in and out as she goaded him, "what if he saw his little virgin, his naughty little girl..... uhhhhh..... fucking her step-brother?"

Mark felt his cock swell with excitement, he'd never heard Hannah talk like this, he thought. Maybe he'd heard her say the word 'dick' on the phone with a girlfriend once or twice, but to hear her talking dirty like that made him fear he might cum right there in her tight pussy.

"He might see me cum inside you then... ughh.... Hannah, you're so tight baby. I don't know how long I can hold on."

"Ummmm... it's... ouhhh... it's fine Mark.... I'm on birth control..." She sounded unconvincing, and she had looked away from him as if to avoid eye contact. He wasn't positive, but he was pretty sure she was smiling.

"Hannah... you're lying, aren't you....?" He questioned her, she put her finger to her lip and nibbled at it naughtily.

"No, I'm not.... Uhhhhh..... don't worry, you can shoot all your cum in me Marky...." She was looking at him through sultry, dazzling eyes.

"Hannah, I can't..." he couldn't help but slide his cock into her one more and continue, "we aren't using protection."

The potion may have helped them get there, but it was Mark's own innocent little step-sis who, now having felt Mark's big cock inside her, wanted nothing but to feel him fill her with his forbidden cum. She knew she was ripe to find herself knocked up by her step-brother, but the thought only excited her. In her mind's eye, she saw Mark fucking her from behind as she stood standing against the wall, waiting until he shot up into her carelessly. So in reality, as he withdrew from her once more, she moved a foot to his pelvis to stop him from skewering her again and to let her get up.

Mark merely watched in awe as his little sister sat up, ABS flexing beautifully, and hopped down from the cart. She walked to the nearby wall and stood with her legs spread apart slightly, so he knew exactly where to put his feet. Just like the image in her head, Mark immediately puts his hands on her body, caressing her sides before taking her hanging breasts in his hands. They were incredibly soft with their weight hanging down into his greedy palms.

But nothing felt as good as that of his cock head, making contact with Hannah's taut, young opening once more. Mark positioned his tip properly and pushed into his beautiful, teenage step-sis, hearing her gasp. As he slid upward into her, the feeling satisfied her dreams more than she could have possibly imagined. It was somehow different, standing in front of her step-brother, completely naked and completely at his mercy.

He'd been worried just before that, and Hannah wanted to put him at ease:

"I want you to fill me up with your sticky cum Mark," Hannah said, pressing her cute butt back toward him to urge his thick cock into her, and then out again as she provoked him, "don't you wanna cum inside me?.....mnnnnghhhhh."

Mark met her hips with his own, a quiet clapping of their flesh emitting from his hastened tempo. He couldn't see them, but the feeling of her glorious tits in his hands, the scent of her thick, dark hair from behind, and the smoothness of her skin had him mesmerized. He could only fuck her harder as he marveled at the beauty of her, in the freckles that kissed her shoulders and the bead of sweat rolling down the flexed arch in her back.

"Fuck me Mark.... Fuck me just like that.... ohhgod..."

What is this feeling that suddenly rushed upon her? All at once she felt short of breath and light headed. Mark could feel her relying on him to hold her up as he thrust into her. Her insides clamped down upon him and he knew what was happening. Hannah was confused and yet deeply enjoying the feeling of her step-brother fucking her from behind.

"What is.....oohohooo Mark... I can't breathe..... ughhh, I feel like I'm gonna.... ooohhh."

Mark pushed her hair across her neck as he cleared a space to kiss her tender skin. He laid one on her, warm and loving, and another, and another -- all moving closer to her ear. Hannah was trying to quiet her cries as Mark manhandled and impaled her from behind with his enormous member.

As she felt his kisses and finally his teeth nibbling at her ear, her body exploded with sensation. It coursed through her veins and flushed from her all but the feeling of Marks rod. Her pussy clamped down even harder, impossibly tight upon him, and try as he might he couldn't contain himself any longer. With only one more withdrawal from his squirming and panting step-sister, her taut channel had him released a first, deep jet of sperm as soon as he had pushed all the way inside her.

"Ohhhhhwwwuuuu...." She howled adorably.

Mark hugged her body tight and tried to keep kissing her. He pumped rope after rope of cum into her fertile womb, so much that she could feel its plentiful warmth inside of her. Mark 's whole body buzzed. He lost himself in a wonderful trance caused by the successful feeling of releasing inside his amazing little step-sister.

Hannah kept quivering long after the last powerful pump of sperm had left her brother's cock. He dared slide an inch or so, out and into her once, so that she shivered and again she whined at the utter sensitivity of her inner walls. He kept doing it, though it was excruciatingly pleasurable for them both, feeling their combined fluids trickling out around his penetrating staff.

"OhmygodSTOP! I can't take it!" Hannah screamed, looking back at him incredulously. She had not yet come all the way down from her heart-wrenching orgasm and couldn't handle any more.

He still felt so enormous inside of her, she wondered if she'd ever recover. Yet she managed to survive even that of Mark's last heedless penetration into her, before he finally came to rest.

She let loose the same smile that she'd revealed after her fake-mad tantrum earlier that day, except this one meant a lot more.

"We're bad Mark," she said, feeling his cock starting to soften inside of her. "I can't believe you came in your own step-sister's pussy!" Suddenly she sounded condemnatory.

"Hannah, I thought you said..." but she cut him off:

"Shhh Mark, I'll give you a pass if you do it again before we have to go back and find Mom and Dad."

His eyes shot to hers, she had finally slid him out of her (though she had to stand on her tiptoes to do it) and was turned to face him. Hannah reached down and took his shaft in her dainty hands; it stopped softening immediately. Mark looked down to see her glistening body, with her round breasts and the most perfect frame he'd ever laid eyes or hands on. He knew then that he'd never say no again.

Hannah kissed her brother so passionately and deeply, standing there in his arms, that he knew their tryst hadn't been all the elixir's doing. Her prying lips and fumbling hands told him how badly she'd wanted him. Mark returned the sentiment, his step-sister with his hands all over her bare skin. The few tender moments allowed both Mark and Hannah to recover, and before long he could tell that his little eighteen-year-old wanted him again.

Mark picked her up by the hips and within moments was fucking her recklessly against the wall. The brick was rough on her naked back, but she'd cared only for the feeling of being fucked again by her step-brother. The cum from their lovemaking minutes earlier only eased the rhythmic immersion of Mark's cock into his beautiful little step-sister.

He humped her against the wall until he could hold her no longer, and then she sat him atop the crate and rode him until they both came again. She thought he might not have it in him, but as she felt another surprising amount of Mark's sperm pumping into her and increasing their risk, she knew she'd been wrong.

After God knows how long the two siblings had somehow gathered themselves enough to try and find their parents. Mark had to smooth back some of Hannah's tussled hair, and once Hannah had to check to be sure her dad wouldn't see a trail of her brother's gleaming spunk coming from the place he'd left it and showing outside her miniature jean shorts. When they finally met back up with their parents, they heard:

"Kids! We've been looking all over for you, we were starting to get worried," said their mom, hugging as they reunited.

"No reason to worry mom, we were doing great on our own." Mark replied

"Oh yeah?" asked his mom, "what did you two get up to today?"

"Only naughty stuff," Hannah said, sounding sarcastic. The look she flashed him, undetected by their oblivious parents, said she knew exactly what she'd meant.

"Ha-ha," finished her brother, "What she means is that we might have gotten shooed away from a hat store for horse-playing, but we found plenty of things to fill up our day.

Hannah's eyes lit a little and she giggled along, "Yeah mom and dad, Mark really helped fill up my day, he's really good at it!"

"I'm glad to hear it you two," said their dad, "for a second there Mark I thought you were going to have your hands full with Hannah in the mood she was in."

They both chortled a little bit, but their parents just figured they were finally getting along, they didn't know how full their son's hands truly had been.

"Yeah, I was in a great mood today for some reason," Hannah went on as her brother's gaze begged her not to say anything more boldly, "Hopefully Mark can help me have a day like this every day this week!"

Mark's imagination ran wild for a few seconds as he thought of all the ways he wanted to explore the perfect little teenager's body. The potion had long since worn off by then. Its effects had been truly gone by the second time they made love, but it left behind something far more significant.

Having broken through the taboo of fucking their own sibling, the potion had allowed Mark and Hannah to take what they'd been denied all along. Neither of the loving siblings could wait to be alone again, so they could once again fuck each other senseless.

As Hannah strode along and walked next to her daddy, bouncing and glancing over her shoulder occasionally at her brother, Mark was entranced. The entire return to the hotel, Mark planned out how he'd somehow maneuver her to a private place so he could wait the absolute minimum amount of time before being buried inside her. Hannah was waiting anxiously for the same thing.

They were undoubtedly in for a hell of a week.

~~The End~~

Here is a preview of another book you may also enjoy:

Captivated & Rekindled Romance

Kerry James

Time Once More
for
Marilyn

Nineteen fifty seven was not a particularly notable year for the world, or for the inhabitants of the United Kingdom. Of course, there were quite a few people who would look back and say. "That was a good year, a very good year." But for many it was just another year. There were births, quite a few into poverty and starvation and the law of averages dictated that an equal number died possibly from that same poverty and starvation.

In October the Soviets would launch the first orbiting satellite and the word 'Sputnik' became part of every language. This was a shock for every developed nation, particularly the Americans, as no one thought that the Russians had the technology to achieve that feat. We all got a year older, although some, like my mother celebrated her birthday and resolutely remained thirty five, ignoring the fact that she was born in nineteen eleven. The Spartan existence, we had known in these isles during WW2 and immediately after had relaxed and our family along with many others was enjoying a more comfortable life.

Our Prime Minister had told us we were never having it so good. At that time, in our innocence we tended to believe the politicians; later the scales would drop from our eyes. For the moment we went along with this fantasy. Most families had a television now and a refrigerator and if those were the yardstick by which to judge then we were indeed better off. There were jobs for all those who wanted to work and State Benefits for those who declined that activity.

The Unions flexed their muscles to introduce socialist principles into Industry. They battled for those whom they called 'the workers' implying by inference that anyone who wasn't unionized was a shirker or a parasite or both. The 'workers' ironically spent more time not working; as their shop stewards frequently called them out on strike for the flimsiest of reasons. The Unions espoused democracy yet rarely let their members vote on strike action. The conflict between the workers and the management was a running battle that went on and on, ensuring years later the almost complete demise of British industry. If we were having it so good, it was a Fool's Paradise. However, for the moment we basked in the sunshine.

It was a surprise, therefore when my dad announced that the family were going away for a week's holiday. The surprise was that I was

From the Author

If you enjoyed any of my books then please share the love and promote my books in Amazon.

If you write me a review and send me an email I will send you a free book, or many.
(Just know that these emails are filtered by my publisher.)

Good news is always welcome.

One Last Thing, For Kindle Readers...

When you turn the page, Kindle will give you the opportunity to rate this book and share your thoughts on Facebook and Twitter. If you enjoyed my writings, would you please take a few seconds to let your friends know about it? Because... when they enjoy they will be grateful to you and so will I.

Thank You!

Michael Fiori
michael_fiori@awesomeauthors.org

included. When I was young, we had family holidays. A week or two in the West Country, travelling there by train with accommodation provided by the euphemistically described 'Guest House'.

A Guest House was one very small step above a boarding house. The furnishings were better, but the rules were the same, whatever the weather you had to leave during the day and not return before five o'clock. You were provided with bed, breakfast, and an evening meal, no early morning or afternoon tea. For me, the journey by train was the highlight. We travelled by 'The Cornish Riviera Express', the crack train of the Great Western, which, in nineteen forty-eight became the Western Region of British Railways. In those days it was still hauled by a steam engine, either a 'King' or 'Castle', gleaming in Brunswick Green with brass trim and copper burnished all glittering in the light. It was supposed to run non-stop to Truro in Cornwall, but it did stop at Plymouth. Not in the station, but just outside so the engine could be changed. The 'Kings' and 'Castles' were too heavy for the Royal Albert Bridge over the Tamar so they were changed for another, lighter locomotive.

It was only later that I understood that during the holiday season there were at least three or four trains that left Paddington in the space of an hour and a half, all called 'The Cornish Riviera Express'. That did mar a little the pride in travelling on that special train. In the mid-fifties, my dad took a new job; moving the whole family from the London area to the Midlands. His position also allowed him a company car for private as well as business use. So the romance of the Cornish Riviera was now history.

To purchase the book, look for **Time Once More for Marilyn.**